captain
FIREBEARD'S
SCHOOL FOR PIRATES

LANCASHIRE COUNTY LIBRARY

D0307862

First published in the UK in 2016 by Scholastic Children's Books
An imprint of Scholastic Ltd
Euston House, 24 Eversholt Street
London, NW1 1DB, UK
Registered office: Westfield Road, Southam, Warwickshire, CV47 0RA
SCHOLASTIC and associated logos are trademarks
and/or registered trademarks of Scholastic Inc.

Text copyright © Chae Strathie, 2016
Illustration copyright © Anna Chernyshova, 2016

The rights of Chae Strathie and Anna Chernyshova to be identified as
the author and illustrator of this work have been asserted by them.

ISBN 978 1407 16339 0

A CIP catalogue record for this book is available from the British Library

All rights reserved.
This book is sold subject to the condition that it shall not, by way of trade
or otherwise, be lent, hired out or otherwise circulated in any form of binding
or cover other than that in which it is published. No part of this publication may be
reproduced, stored in a retrieval system, or transmitted in any form or by any means
(electronic, mechanical, photocopying, recording or otherwise) without the
prior written permission of Scholastic Limited.

Printed in Malaysia
Papers used by Scholastic Children's Books are made
from wood grown in sustainable forests.

1 3 5 7 9 10 8 6 4 2

This is a work of fiction. Names, characters, places, incidents and dialogues
are products of the author's imagination or are used fictitiously. Any resemblance
to actual people, living or dead, events or locales is entirely coincidental.

www.scholastic.co.uk

Lancashire Library Services	
30118133948855	
PETERS	JF
£5.99	02-Mar-2017
CPP	

WRITTEN BY
CHAE STRATHIE

ILLUSTRATED BY
ANNA CHERNYSHOVA

Captain
FIREBEARD'S
SCHOOL FOR PIRATES

SCHOLASTIC

*With love to Cap'n Pete
and Cap'n Catriona
– may your voyage through
life together be a long and
happy one, me hearties!*

X X

CHAPTER 1

"NNNNNNGGGG MMMMRRR GAAH!"

said Tommy.

But no matter how hard he tried, he just could not squeeze a beard out.

All around him fierce-looking men with hairy forests on their faces glared down from pictures hung on his bedroom walls.

There was Captain Bluebeard…

Captain Squarebeard…

Captain Birdbeard…

Captain Weirdbeard…

Captain Spikebeard…

And Captain Wildbeard.

They were Tommy's favourite pirates.

But his *favourite* favourite pirate was Captain Firebeard, headmaster of Captain Firebeard's School for Pirates – and today was Tommy's first day in class.

If only he could squeeze out a magnificent beard before school started at nine o'clock he was sure he'd impress Captain Firebeard and get a whole bunch of pirate points right away.

He checked the mirror.

There wasn't even one measly whisker on his chin.

Not. A. Sausage. (Although he'd have been quite surprised if he'd managed to squeeze a sausage out of his chin.)

"Hurry up, dear!" called his mum from downstairs. "You'll be late if we don't leave now."

Tommy straightened his red spotty neckerchief and made sure his white-and-black-striped school tunic was shipshape and correct. Then he had a quick look in his school bag to make sure he had everything he needed.

✔ *Captain Firebeard's Introduction To Pirating*: check.

✔ Grandpa Jack's compass: check.

✔ Swimming trunks and goggles in case he had to walk the plank: check.

✔ A Jolly Roger pencil case: check.

✔ Two pieces of eight for the tuck shop: check.

He buckled the bag and dashed out

the door … then dashed straight back in again.

He'd almost forgotten the most important thing – his letter of invitation to join Captain Firebeard's Pirate School.

No letter – no entry. Them's the rules! read a warning written in red at the bottom of the letter.

Mum and Dad were waiting at the door.

"Come on, lad," said Dad. "Your

timbers will be well and truly shivered if you're late on your first day."

"You know what they say about Captain Firebeard, don't you?" said Mum.

"Fiery of beard, fiery of temper," gulped Tommy. "Thanks for reminding me, Mum."

They lived within a seagull's squawk of the docks where the school was,

so it would only take
five minutes to walk
there. Tommy glanced
at the clock tower
that rose above the
higgledy-piggledy roofs.
Six minutes to nine.
They'd have to be quick.

As they hurried towards the harbour Tommy's tummy was rising and falling like a rowing boat in a hurricane. He'd never been so nervous in his life.

They rounded the final corner just as the clock struck nine. There in front of them was the *Rusty Barnacle* – or Captain Firebeard's School For Pirates, as it was also known.

The ship is certainly well named, thought Tommy. There was plenty of rust, and even more barnacles.

The hull was covered in peeling red paint, and three masts rose from the deck. What looked like a tree house was perched precariously high on top of the main mast. It was also a bit, well, bulgy. An unusual shape compared to the normal ships next to it.

Odd bits and bobs had been added to it here and there – extra rooms with wonky windows that jutted out from the sides of the ship at weird angles, and an enormous home-made

telescope that looked like it had been made from a variety of glass jars, pipes, dustbins and a battered tuba.

The last bong of the clock rang out across the harbour.

"Phew," said Tommy. "Just made it."

They hurried over to the gangplank.

"Now, remember to wash behind your ears," fussed Mum.

"Yes, Mum," said Tommy.

"And don't play with any cannons," said Dad.

"No, Dad," said Tommy.

"Be good," said Mum, sniffling into a yellow hanky.

"Be **FEARSOME!**" said Dad.

Tommy stopped at the gangplank.

"Bye, Mum. Bye, Dad," he said. "I'll see you at the end of term."

They hugged each other and Tommy turned and joined the other children boarding the *Rusty Barnacle*. He noticed worried-looking faces all around him. One small lad in particular looked like he was about to be seasick – and he wasn't even on the ship yet!

A pointy-faced boy had used his sharp elbows to push right to the front of the line. His pirate uniform looked expensive and very elaborate. Tommy didn't much like the look of him.

Someone nudged Tommy's arm.

"Hurry up, landlubber," said a girl's

voice. "Let's get on with the adventure!"

Tommy turned to see a redheaded girl fiddling with her ponytail. Her red spotty headscarf matched her neckerchief. She had a fearless sparkle in her eyes. She would either be a lot of fun … or a lot of trouble.

He smiled nervously and trotted on up the gangplank.

Even though the boat was a rickety old bucket, Tommy was proud to be aboard. Only a handful of young buccaneers got chosen each year to be taken on board the best pirate school on the Seven Seas – and now he was one of them.

He joined the crowd of new pupils who were standing around, wondering what to do next when …

CREEEEAAAAAAKKKKK

A door opened in the wall of the quarterdeck in front of them.

Everyone stared.

A gleaming metal hook appeared and pushed the door open further.

"AAAARRRRRRRRRRR,"

came a throaty voice from the darkness. "Welcome aboard, lads and lasses. Captain Firebeard's School For Pirates now be in session."

CHAPTER 2

The gleaming hook turned out to be connected to an arm, which was connected to a pirate.

"My name be Sea Dog Steve," the pirate growled. "And I be Captain Firebeard's right-hand man."

More like right-hook man, thought Tommy.

"Now, you landlubbing whelks," continued the pirate. "Without further ado, let me introduce your teachers. First, we 'ave One-Eyed Norm – the crackest of crack shots and a dab hand with a cutlass. He can hit a gold doubloon from a mile away and slice a coconut in two with his good eye shut!"

"AAARRRRRRRRRR!" said One-Eyed Norm, who had a large green patch over his right eye.

"**AᴬARᴿRᴿRᴿRᴿRRR!**" replied Sea Dog Steve.

"**Aarrrꜛꜛ,**" piped up a small voice from the crowd of pupils.

"Oi!" said Sea Dog Steve. "No '**AᴬRᴿRᴿRᴿRᴿR**-ing' until you've been taught how to '**AᴬRᴿRᴿRᴿR**' properly."

"Sorry, sir," said the small voice.

"Next we have Maggie Magpie," continued Sea Dog Steve. "She's got an eye for treasure and a nose for adventure. Best keep a close watch on

yer pieces of eight when she's around."

"HA-HAAR!" yelled Maggie Magpie as she swung down on a rope, did a somersault and landed next to Sea Dog Steve.

"Hallo, me hearties," she laughed.

Sea Dog Steve smiled to reveal a shiny gold tooth gleaming in his mouth. His chin was so stubbly he could have used it to sand the deck smooth and his eyes were as green as the leaves on a palm tree.

Next he gestured towards a hatch in the deck. "Every ship needs a great ship's cook," he said. "Unfortunately, we be stuck with Gumms."

"Well, sizzle my sausages, we be awash with shrimplets!" wheezed Gumms, opening the hatch and letting out a pong that smelled like he'd been boiling fish heads and smelly socks in cabbage water.

"What's for lunch, Gumms?" shouted Sea Dog Steve.

"Fish heads and smelly socks in cabbage water," chortled Gumms.

"Can't wait," winced Sea Dog Steve. "And finally," he added dramatically, "a legend what don't need no introduction."

He pointed upwards to the deck above, and there, looking down at everyone from beside the ship's wheel, was Captain Firebeard himself!

Tommy felt a thrill run through him. His hero was right in front of him, complete with crimson jacket, shiny gold cutlass, wooden leg and crutch … and a mighty beard the colour of flame.

"Welcome to my school," he bellowed. "You all be pirate pupils now, and we're going to turn you into the best buccaneers on the high seas! So if there be any snivelling sea cucumbers or lolloping limpet lickers here, I suggest you jump ashore quick."

Then he drew his curved cutlass and thwacked a big brass bell with it.

BOOONNNG!

That seemed to be the signal to set sail, and with a creak of wood and a ripple of sails the *Rusty Barnacle* slowly moved away from the harbour wall and began its journey out to sea.

There was a clamour of cheers and tears from the port as the crowd of mums and dads and grannies and granddads hooted their goodbyes.

"Show the pupils to their quarters – then let the classes begin!

"AAARRRRRRRRR!"

Captain Firebeard barked, then he turned and stomp-clomped out of sight.

"Follow me, young spratlings," said Sea Dog Steve.

He led the class through a hatch in the deck and down some wooden stairs. They walked through the cannon deck, where a pair of odd-looking pirates – one tall and thin and one short and round – were polishing cannonballs.

Next they passed a small sailor with hairy feet testing a plank by walking off it into a bathtub.

The classroom was down a crooked corridor. There was a sign on the door that read:

PIRATES IN TRAINING –
NO LANDLUBBERS, BILGE RATS
OR SCURVY SEA WEASELS!

Then they came to the canteen. The smell from Gumms's cooking was strong enough to strip the varnish off a wooden leg.

"I think I'm going to faint," gasped the small lad who'd looked very seasick earlier.

"Best give that little 'un a helping hand," said Sea Dog Steve to Tommy.

Tommy grabbed the boy's arm to hold him up. The girl who'd

nudged him on the gangplank took his other arm.

"I'm Jo," she said. "Definitely NOT Josephine, no matter what anyone says. Right?"

"Err, right," said Tommy. "I'm Tommy. Definitely not Josephine either."

The small boy groaned as the ship rolled from side to side on a wave. "And I'm … probably going to be sick. Oh, and my name's Milton."

Sea Dog Steve pointed towards another staircase.

"Your quarters be down there," he said. "Choose a hammock and get your belongings squared away, then be in the classroom in ten minutes."

Before anyone got a chance to move, the spiky boy with the expensive outfit barged through, pushing people out of the way and almost knocking Milton to the floor.

"That's Spencer Splinter," scowled

Jo. "He thinks he's the best thing since sliced fishcakes just because Captain Blackbeard was his granddad. Watch out for him – he's as prickly as a hedgehog wrapped in nettles, and as slippery as an eel in a barrel of butter."

By the time Tommy and Jo had helped Milton down the stairs there were only three hammocks left.

"Looks like these are our quarters," said Tommy, putting his belongings in a locker next to his hammock.

"Aye aye to that, shipmates!" smiled
Jo.

"Yo-ho-ho," said Milton weakly.

It was time to start pirating!

CHAPTER 3

On the way to the classroom Milton made sure he held his nose when they went through the canteen.

As usual, Spencer and his two friends – a massive boy who looked like a great white shark in a pirate outfit and a girl with the grumpiest face in the universe – elbowed their

way to the front. Spencer gave Tommy
a good dig in the ribs on the way past.

Captain Firebeard and Sea Dog Steve were waiting for them.

"Welcome to the classroom," said Captain Firebeard. "This be your home for the rest of the term."

Tommy's tummy did a funny little somersault followed by a roly-poly that had nothing to do with the rocking ship. He still couldn't quite believe he was actually a pupil at the best pirate school there was – or that he was in the same room as the star of his bedroom-wall posters.

The classroom was very old-fashioned. It had wooden desks and rickety old chairs. On each desk was a brass compass, a pot of ink and a big feathered quill to write with.

There were maps and navigational charts pinned to the wooden walls alongside diagrams of cannons and guides to different types of treasure. At the front of the room was a blackboard and a large desk for the

teacher. Beside that was a row of wooden perches, each one with a brightly coloured parrot sitting on it.

An excited buzz went round the classmates as they tried to guess which one of the birds would be assigned to each of them.

"Now," continued Captain Firebeard, "before we begin any lessons, we need to furnish you all with lovely new pirate names. It wouldn't be proper to be callin' yourself Nigel or Tabitha when you could be named something like Crow's Nest Nige or Tabby the Terrible."

He nodded to Sea Dog Steve, who picked up a pile of papers from the teacher's desk.

"We've been checking your school application forms," said Sea Dog Steve, "and we've come up with some howlin' good pirate names for you all."

He examined the first piece of paper.

"You there – Jo, lass," he said. "You're a proper wild-heart, so your new name be Jo the Fearless."

Jo punched the air. "Yes! Love it!"
she yelped.

"And you," he said pointing to
Milton. "It was going to be Brains,

bein' as you're proper clever, but after this morning's wibbly-wobbly hoo-hah, it be Jellylegs from now on."

Milton sighed.

"The pointy lad," he went on, nodding at Spencer. "You be Spiky Spencer, as you looks as sharp as a bag o' needles and pins!"

Captain Firebeard guffawed loudly at this. Spencer did not.

"Do you know who my grandfather was?" snapped Spencer. "He was Blackbeard himself!"

Captain Firebeard's bright red beard bristled.

"That he may have been, laddie," he

said sternly. "But this 'ere be Captain

FIREBEARD'S

school, not Captain Blackbeard's school. Spiky Spencer it is."

Spencer looked annoyed, but stayed silent as his two cronies were named Muttonhead Max and Greta the Grouch.

When all the names were given out except one, it was finally Tommy's turn.

Sea Dog Steve lifted the piece of paper.

"Ah, yes," he smiled. "Top in the pirateology entry test. Seems we 'ave a bit of a star in the making, Captain."

"We'll see about that," said Captain Firebeard, stroking his crimson bristles. "Let's call you Hotshot Tom – see if you can live up to yer new name, eh?"

Tommy felt his cheeks go the same colour as Captain Firebeard's whiskers.

"Y-yes, sir," he stammered.

"Aye aye, sir, ye mean," said Captain Firebeard.

"Yes. I mean, aye, sir. And another aye," blustered Tommy.

With the naming ceremony over, Sea Dog Steve crossed to where the parrots were waiting.

One by one he called the pirate pupils forward by their new names and introduced them to their feathered friends.

Jo got a vibrant blue-and-red parrot called Flash, who had a big white lightning bolt on the front of his puffed-out chest.

Milton got a small, pale yellow parrot called Wobbles, who refused to sit on his shoulder because it was scared of heights.

Spencer's parrot was off sick after scoffing some of Gumms's octopus porridge, so he got a scrawny crow called Scratcher instead.

When Sea Dog Steve called out, "Your turn, Hotshot," Tommy went to the front of the class.

Sea Dog Steve lifted a bright green bird from its perch and placed it on Tommy's shoulder.

"Meet Cheeky McBeaky," said the pirate. "He's a bit of a smart alec. Good luck."

Tommy looked at Cheeky McBeaky. Cheeky McBeaky looked at Tommy.

"Can I get another one?"

squawked the parrot. "**This one looks a wee bit dim.**"

Captain Firebeard ignored him.

"Right, you shower of sea urchins!" he roared. "Into yer seats. Lessons is about to BEGIN!"

And with that he strode out the room in a flurry of scarlet.

CHAPTER 4

First lesson of the day was How To Speak Like A Pirate. Sea Dog Steve stood in front of the class.

"Let's start nice and easy, me buckos," he said. "Everyone repeat after me – 'AHOY, ME HEARTIES!'"

"AHOY, ME HEARTIES!" chanted the class.

"Now, can anyone tell me what that means?" said Sea Dog Steve.

Half the class put their hands up.

"It means 'Hello there, my friends'," shouted out Spencer. "Every idiot knows that."

Sea Dog Steve fixed him with a glare.

"You puts your hand up when you be answerin' a question, lad," he growled. "Once, when I was in school, I didn't put my hand up … and look what happened to me." He held up his shiny hook.

Spencer gulped and looked at his hand nervously. Sea Dog Steve winked at the rest of the class then turned and wrote on the board.

"Now, you'll all be needing to speak proper if you wants to be real pirates one day. So let's all say these good old phrases together," he said. He pointed to each line in turn and the class chorused them out loud.

"SHIVER ME TIMBERS."

"SING US A SHANTY."

"PASS ME SPYGLASS."

"AVAST, ME HEARTY."

"YOU SOGGY BILGE RAT."

"Yo-ho-ho."

"Where did I bury me plunder?"

"SWAB THE POOP DECK."

A girl at the back started giggling at that one.

"There be nothing funny about 'poop deck'," said Sea Dog Steve. Several other children started giggling when he said the word again.

Sea Dog Steve sighed. "Right, class, get it out yer system.

POOP, POOP, POOPITY- POOP, POOOOOOOOOOOOOP, POOPY-POOPY, POOPTY-DOO, POOP!"

The whole class was crying with laughter by this point.

"I thinks that's enough pirate talk for today," muttered Sea Dog Steve. "Tomorrow I be teaching you how to do a right good 'AᴬᴬᴬARʀʀRʀRʀʀR.' Now, up on deck with ye, you jabbering jellyfish!"

The class filed out with their parrots on their shoulders, still chuckling.

Up on the gently rolling deck Maggie Magpie was waiting for them.

"AHOY, ME HEARTIES!"

she called as spray from a wave splashed behind her.

"AHOY!"

replied the class in unison.

"Oooo, I see you've been learning pirate-speak," she said. "Most impressive. But let's see if you're as good at climbing."

Maggie pointed at Milton.

"You go first, me lad," she said.

"You're as small as a prawn – you should be able to scamper up to the crow's nest in quick smart time."

She pointed to the very top of the tallest mast on the ship. Milton shielded his eyes as he followed her finger. He could see a small wooden speck high above. It seemed an awful long way away.

He started quivering … then trembling … then shaking like a jelly on a washing machine.

Without warning Muttonhead Max gave him an almighty shove from behind and Milton flew on to the rigging.

"Crackling cuttlefish! That's the spirit!" said Maggie, who hadn't seen the push. "Look how keen he is! Up ye go, laddie."

Milton gingerly climbed one square of rigging at a time.

"Too high! Too high!" squawked Wobbles the parrot, who

had finally plucked up the courage to sit on Milton's shoulder at precisely the wrong moment. "**Oh no! We're going to fall! Definitely going to plummet!**" He jumped on to Milton's face and wrapped his wings around his head in terror.

Milton couldn't see a thing and clung to the ropes for dear life, despite being only knee-high off the ground.

Maggie gently lifted him down.

Next it was Tommy's turn. He did better. But halfway up his parrot, McBeaky, piped up, "**Squawk!** Here's a funny joke."

"Not now, McBeaky," said Tommy.

But McBeaky carried on. "Why are pirates called pirates?" he screeched. "They just **aaaaarrrrrrrr! HA HA HA! SQUAAAWK!**"

A parrot cackling its little feathery beak off right in your ear is enough to put anyone off climbing rigging,

and Tommy was no different. As he reached for the next square of rope he missed it completely and tumbled all the way to the bottom, where Maggie caught him just in time.

Spencer pushed his way to the front. "I'll be great at this," he declared

and launched himself at the ropes.
Unfortunately he was so sharp and
spiky that his elbows sliced the rigging
and he hurtled straight through and
landed head first in a pile of leftover
fishy slops that Gumms had thrown
out. Yuk!

Maggie sighed. "Aren't *any* of you good at clambering?"

Jo stepped forward confidently. She eyed the rigging, took a deep breath … did three forward flips and bounced high on to the ropes.

She scuttled up like a monkey, swinging, springing and leaping up to the crow's nest tree house in the blink of an eye.

"Top of the class," chuckled Maggie Magpie. "In more ways than one."

After that it was down to the cannon deck for target practice with One-Eyed Norm. Instead of real cannonballs they used big, round custard doughnuts.

Jellylegs Milton got such a fright from the loud bangs that he and Wobbles hid inside a coil of rope.

Spencer's crow, Scratcher, pecked his doughnut to crumbs before he even had the chance to load it.

Jo was so keen to have a go that she

didn't take her time at all and blasted
the captain of a passing pirate ship
full in the face with a massive splurge

of custard. He was not pleased. Getting custard out of a beard is a

By the time everyone had their turn there was custard and bits of doughnut everywhere. But not a drop on the target floating off the port side.

"Well, our enemies won't have much to worry about," said One-Eyed Norm, wiping a blob of yellow gloop out of his good eye.

Tommy was last to go. He loaded his cannon carefully. Aimed precisely. Told McBeaky to stop telling silly jokes. Closed his eyes, just like One-

Eyed Norm did when he'd shown
them what to do, aaaand …

BANG!

SPLAT!

Bullseye.

"Well, shiver me timbers!" exclaimed One-Eyed Norm. "Looks like we got a natural on our hands, eh, Hotshot Tom?"

"Teacher's pet," whispered Spencer.

But Tommy wasn't listening. He was too busy imagining what he'd look like with a big pirate captain's beard to care about what Spiky Spencer said.

CHAPTER 5

After days of classes on things like how to walk the gangplank gracefully, beginners' cutlass swishing, Jolly Roger flag hoisting and how to shout "AAARRRRRRR!" like a pro, the pupils were starting to get into the swing of things.

One morning, after a particularly

disgusting breakfast of kipper porridge and boiled seaweed, Tommy, Jo and Milton headed to the classroom for their first pirate history lesson.

Captain Firebeard himself was taking the class that morning.

A screen had been set up at the front of the room and a rickety old oil-powered projector was resting on a table at the back.

"Switch off them lights, Blaze,"

said Captain Firebeard to his bright red parrot.

"Aye aye, Captain," squawked the bird as it flew over and pecked the light switch.

The room was plunged into darkness, until the projector flickered to life.

"Right, class," said Captain Firebeard. "Here is a quick history of pirates from the earliest times. First, in the days of the cavemen pirates, was Captain Stonebeard."

The slide on the screen showed a picture of a pirate with a wooden cutlass, a very rocky looking beard and a pterodactyl sitting on his shoulder instead of a parrot.

"Then, in Ancient Egyptian times, there was Captain Bootankhamun."

The picture changed to show a pirate with big gold buccaneer boots and a pharaoh's hat.

Then there came the Roman pirate, Captain Beardus Maximus…

And the Viking pirate, Captain Axebeard…

And the Pirates of the Round Table…

And finally the great explorer pirate, Captain Wanderbeard, who discovered the famous pirate haven of Plunderossa.

As each of the images appeared, Captain Firebeard told the class all about the history of each pirate and the pupils wrote down notes in their jotters using their feather quills and inkwells.

"Lights on, Blaze," ordered Captain Firebeard when they came to the end of the slides. "Now, let me tell you about some of the most bruising, blazing battles ever fought on the seven seas."

He opened a cabinet in the corner and, with a dramatic flourish, whipped out an enormous silver cutlass.

The class oOo-ed.

"This be the very cutlass used by Captain Nastybeard in the Battle of Screaming and Running Away a Lot, in which he caused lots of other pirates to scream and run away a lot on account of him being very nasty and having this big cutlass here."

The class drew a picture of the cutlass in their books.

"And this be an actual cannonball used in the Battle of Squashed Nose," said Captain Firebeard. "And if you look carefully, you can still sec the dent in the shape of a nose, what was

made when it hit Captain Eggbeard
… or Captain Flatface, as he now be
known."

McBeaky, who was sitting on Tommy's shoulder, screeched with laughter at that. "Captain Flatface! Ha, ha! Squawk! Good one!"

"Simmer down, parrot," said Captain Firebeard. "Now, does anyone have any questions?"

"When will we be talking about Captain Blackbeard?" shouted Spencer, without putting his hand up. "The greatest pirate who ever lived!"

Captain Firebeard's red beard bristled.

"We might save him for the lesson on pirates what got too big for their beards," he said, scowling.

Spencer looked annoyed and muttered something about "telling his father all about this".

Just then Tommy noticed something on the wall beside him. It was a map of an island, but underneath it were several lines of peculiar pictures, symbols and letters.

He put his hand up.

"Yes, Hotshot?" said Captain Firebeard.

"What's this weird map all about,

sir?" asked Tommy.

Captain Firebeard clumped across the room on his wooden leg to where the map was. The class crowded round to see.

"This," said Captain Firebeard in a hushed tone, "be the Mysterious Map of Mandaloo. It is said to reveal the way to a secret island – Skull Island – on which be buried a lost chest of the most magnificent treasure any pirate has ever seen."

The eyes of every pupil were as wide and round as cannonballs.

"But why did no one ever go and get the treasure?" asked Jo.

"Because the directions be in some sort of code," said the Captain. "And we pirates aren't known for our code-breaking skills, so it has remained undiscovered for hundreds of years. Right, that be enough lessons for now. Time for a break. Off ye go."

The pupils hustled and bustled out

of the door leaving the classroom empty.

All except for Milton, who was standing alone staring at the map.

"Hmmm," he said quietly. "I wonder…"

CHAPTER 6

Learning to be a pirate is tiring work.

So after a long day of advanced yo-ho-ho-ing, vigorous poop deck polishing and desperately trying to squeeze beards out (even Jo) it was no wonder all the pupils were fast asleep in their hammocks.

Even Muttonhead Max's thunderous snore, which was so loud it rattled the wooden deck above, couldn't wake them.

The ship had sailed back to the harbour in town to tie up for the night and, in-between snores, all was dark and still, with only a single flickering lantern for light. The parrots were snoozing on their perches (except for Wobbles who was so afraid of heights he slept in a shoebox on the floor with a hot-water bottle to keep him warm).

Tommy was dreaming.

In his dream he had a bushy red beard, just like Captain Firebeard's. All of the other pupils were *soooo* jealous – especially Spencer, who had an embarrassingly tiny mousey-brown beard with only three weedy wisps on it.

But suddenly the beard began to grow. And grow. And GROW! Before long it covered everything in sight.

Tommy was just a tiny face in the middle of a vast beardy sea.

"Wake up, Tommy!" hissed Jo.

"GAH! BIG BEARD IN MY FACE!" spluttered Tommy, waking with a start.

"What?" said Jo.

"Oh, err, nothing," said Tommy. "What in the name of Neptune's big toe are you doing?"

Jo was standing between Tommy and Milton's hammocks. She was dressed in full pirate kit.

Tommy rubbed his eyes and yawned. "Please tell me we don't have to do lessons at night as well," he groaned.

"Don't be silly," said Jo. "I have a plan."

"I was worried you'd say that," sighed Milton sitting up blearily. "Middle-of-the-night plans are my least favourite kind of plans."

"Go on then," said Tommy. "What's your big idea?"

"Well," said Jo. "You know that map we saw earlier?"

"Yes," said Tommy.

"The secret treasure one?"

"Yes."

"The one with the code?"

"I totally know the map!" said Tommy. "Get on with it!"

"Well, I say we 'borrow' it, take the ship and find the treasure," said Jo. "Whaddaya think?" She smiled encouragingly.

Milton pulled the covers over his head and mumbled, "Go back to bed."

Tommy rolled his eyes. "It's a daft idea!" he said. "There's no way it would work."

"It so would," said Jo, putting her hands on her hips defiantly. "So how about we put what we've learned to good use and actually start acting like pirates?'"

"No. Way," said Tommy. "We'd get caught and thrown out of school. Or made to walk the plank into shark-infested water. Or fired out of a cannon into a giant squid's bottom. Or all three."

Jo looked annoyed for a moment. Then a smile appeared on her face as she thought of something. She reached across to Tommy's locker and picked up his copy of *Captain Firebeard's Introduction To Pirating*. Flicking through the pages, she quickly found what she was looking for.

"Aha!" she exclaimed. "Here it is." She read a passage from the book out loud, "If a friendly pirate asks his or her shipmates to go on a treasure-hunting mission, the Pirate's Code of Conduct states that they must accept the request immediately with no grumbling, backsliding or hiding under blankets like a lily-livered landlubber."

Tommy scratched his chin. Milton pulled the covers off his head.

"She's right, you know," said Tommy. "We have to go."

Milton sighed, but swung his legs out of his hammock.

They pulled on their waistcoats and neckerchiefs and gently woke up their parrots. Then the three of them sneaked ever so quietly past their fellow pupils and tiptoed up the stairs.

When they reached the top they turned the corner … and came face to face with Sea Dog Steve sitting on a chair next to the canteen! They almost jumped out of their boots.

snored Sea Dog Steve.

He was in a deep, deep sleep.

So were Maggie Magpie,

One-Eyed Norm and Gumms.

It looked like they'd been enjoying a little too much grog after dinner.

"Phew," whispered Jo.

They crept to the classroom and opened the door slowly. Inside, all was in shadow. A wedge of light from the open door stretched across the room and up the far wall. And there, in its dark wooden frame, was the Mysterious Map of Mandaloo.

Milton gulped.

Tommy took a deep breath.

Jo stepped into the room and said,

**"Come on me hearties
- let's find us
some treasure!"**

CHAPTER 7

Getting hold of a mysterious treasure map is one thing … cracking a top-secret code that has foxed pirates for hundreds of years is quite another.

Jo squinted at the map. Tommy scratched the back of his head. McBeaky tried peering at it upside down.

Wobbles didn't like the look of it so he hid under a hat.

Flash flew round it five times then pecked it for good measure. Since it was now out of the frame and flattened out on a desk, all this did was give Flash a sore beak and a headache.

Only Milton looked relaxed about the whole thing. And Milton **NEVER** looked relaxed.

He leaned back in a chair and smiled.

"What are you looking so happy about?" asked Tommy. "We've got a code to break and you're not being much help."

Milton winked at him.

"Winking won't do any good," said Jo. "Solving. That's what we need."

Milton yawned.

"That slippery sea monkey knows something," said Tommy. "Look at his face!"

"Milto-o-o-o-n," said Jo.

"What do you know?"

Milton got up and crossed to the desk where the map lay.

"The code," said Milton triumphantly, "is easy. You just have to know how to read it."

Everyone gazed at the random symbols, letters and numbers below the map.

"Nope," said Tommy eventually. "Not seeing it."

"Not. A. Thing," murmured Jo.

Milton pointed to the first set of symbols.

"Look," he said. "The letter S plus a picture of a tail with the letter T scored out. What does that make?"

"My head hurt?" said Jo.

"It makes the word 'sail' once you add it all together. Then there's a number two – 'Sail to…'. Do you see?"

"Ahhh, I get it now," said Tommy. "Let's work out the rest."

(Turn to the back of the book
to see how Tommy, Milton
and Jo cracked the code!)

"We've done it!" yelped Jo. "Milton, you're a GENIUS!"

Tommy high-fived a beaming Milton. Even McBeaky seemed impressed.

"Now all we need to do is get to Skull Island," said Tommy.

Milton's face fell. Solving the code was the easy part – going on a risky mission to a mysterious island was a whole different kettle of fish fingers.

"There's only one way to get there,"

said Jo. "Follow me."

Milton rolled up the map and they scurried out of the room and crept past the sleeping teachers.

Up the stairs they went, out on to the deck. Then they made a beeline for the ship's wheel.

"I'll untie the rope and you steer," said Jo to Tommy. "Milton, you keep lookout."

"A-are you sure about this?" stammered Milton.

As Jo leaped away to untie the ship from the dockside, Tommy positioned himself gingerly behind the big wooden wheel. It was almost the same size as him. He'd never steered a ship before. Suddenly this pirating business seemed extremely real.

Even Jo felt a bit nervous – although she'd never have admitted it.

The sound of a heavy rope splashing into water could be heard, and then the boat slowly began to move.

"Hoist a sail, Jo!" hissed Tommy as quietly as he could.

A moment later one of the sails rose up the mast with a rustle.

A gust of wind caught it and it billowed, sending the ship surging forward … straight for a tugboat.

"Oh, crabsticks!" yelped Tommy as he yanked the wheel hard.

It was as heavy as could be, but he just managed to brush past the tug's bows with a catfish's whisker to spare.

"That was close," he chuckled.

A wooden cruise-liner that was ten times the size of the *Rusty Barnacle* blasted its horn not far from Tommy's head as they skimmed just inches apart, blowing him clean off his feet.

When he got up off the deck his hair was sticking straight up in the air.

"Pay attention!" said Jo.

Thankfully the din didn't wake anyone below deck and Tommy managed to steer the ship in a wobbly fashion towards the open sea.

"That's more like it," said Tommy, trying to stand in an impressively piratey way and gaze ahead with his hand shielding his eyes – even though it was night-time and there was no sun.

"What's that funny noise?" said Milton.

Sure enough there was a strange bumping and scraping sound behind the boat.

Jo dashed to the stern of the *Rusty Barnacle*.

"Did anyone raise the anchor?" she shouted.

"Errr," everyone said at once.

"That'll be why we're currently dragging thirteen lobster creels,

five rowing boats and a very upset fisherman behind us then," she said. "Oops. No. Scratch that. The fisherman's gone. Sorry, sir. Hope you catch a mackerel soon."

Tommy shrugged. There was nothing they could do now.

"Look," said Milton. "We're past the harbour walls."

"Next stop, Skull Island," said Jo. "Booty ahoy!"

CHAPTER 8

The *Rusty Barnacle* didn't go near whirlpools much any more – mainly because bits tended to fall off it when it did.

But that night it was heading for the biggest of the lot.

Using an ancient sea chart he found at the bottom of the map chest next to the ship's wheel, Tommy steered the ship in the direction of the Great Whirlpool. McBeaky read out directions while Tommy handled the huge wooden wheel.

"After eighty waves go left at the next sandbank," squawked the parrot. "Then veer right for ten leagues."

After a while a sound could be heard, even over the crash of the waves. It was a low rumbling, growling roar … and it was getting louder.

And **LOUDER.**

"I think we might have arrived," muttered Tommy.

Milton let out a small shriek from his lookout post.

"Yep," said Tommy. "We've arrived."

The Great Whirlpool was as wide as a hundred football pitches and as deep as the ocean itself. At its centre was a great dark swirl, and all round its edges the sea churned and frothed like milkshake in a blender.

Tommy tried desperately to steer around the whirlpool, but the *Rusty Barnacle* hurtled straight towards the raging waters.

"YIKES!" he shouted, "I'm not all that keen on treasure, now I think about it."

Milton screamed and pulled his stripy tunic over his face so he didn't have to see what was going on. Jo gasped and clung to the rigging as the current dragged them into the vortex.

"HOLD ON TIGHT!"

Tommy shouted over the roar.

The boat was sucked into the whirlpool. Round and round it went. Faster and faster. Great walls of water splashed over the hull, drenching Tommy, Jo and Milton and their parrots.

"Och, I just had a bath last Tuesday!" grumbled McBeaky.

The ship spiralled in a vast circle

round the edge of the whirlpool. Any minute now they'd be sucked down into the inky blackness.

"Look!" said Tommy, pointing at a shipwreck just visible in the distance. "Isn't that the next point on the map?"

As they whizzed round, Jo and Milton could just see an old ship jammed against a rock beyond the whirlpool.

"We need to get out of this," said Tommy. In a flash he had an idea.

"Milton, Jo, parrots – come and help me," he said. "I can't turn the wheel by myself."

They rushed over and clung on. As the shipwreck came into view Tommy yelled, **"NOW!"** Everyone pulled as hard as they could, but the wheel didn't budge.

"Hang on," said Tommy. "Where's Wobbles?"

"Squawk! Hiding in a teapot," croaked Flash.

The shipwreck came back round again.

"NOW!" shouted Tommy. They all yanked hard. Nothing.

"we'Re DooMeD!" cried Milton.

Suddenly, with a flap and flutter, Wobbles appeared and landed on the wheel.

"Wobbles needs a hug," he squawked at Milton.

The weight of the trembling parrot

was just enough to tip the balance
and the wheel spun round. The ship
lurched to one side and was launched
out of the whirlpool at high speed.

It flew high through the air like
a boat-shaped jet plane, heading
straight for the old shipwreck.
Everyone closed their eyes.

The Rusty Barnacle landed right
on the end of the semi-sunken ship's
massive mast, which bent … and bent
… and b-e-e-e-e-nt … until:

INNGGGG!

It sprang back and hurled the ship
across the sky to the right.

"Woo-Hoo!"

yelled Jo. "This is the life. We're sky pirates!"

Despite feeling thoroughly sick, Milton was trying his best to cuddle Wobbles while reading the map, which was flapping and twisting in the wind.

"If this is right, Skull Island should be just down th—"

SPLASH!

They landed in the sea again and came to a halt that sent them sprawling.

When they picked themselves up they peered over the wheel.

"Skull Island," they gasped in unison.

All was still once again … and the three friends smiled at each other when they heard a reassuringly loud snore echo up a hatch from down below. Thankfully the crew of the

Rusty Barnacle were used to rough seas and stormy oceans, so they could sleep through anything.

The only question now was how they were going to get from the ship to the island.

They were racking their brains when McBeaky squawked, **"Spaghetti!"**

"This is no time for a snack," said Tommy.

"Spaghetti!" McBeaky screeched again, flapping over to a barrel.

Of course! Gumms had made the toughest spaghetti in the history of the universe for dinner. And there was a barrel-load right there on deck.

"Come on," said Tommy. "Let's get tying and we can make a zip wire."

So they all delved into the barrel and began tying the rubbery spaghetti together to make a long rope. When they were done, they tied one end to the main mast and Flash took the other end in his beak and flew to

the island where he tied it round a coconut tree.

"Quick," said Jo. "Let's go before anyone wakes up."

They stood on the side of the ship and looped their neckerchiefs over the spaghetti rope. Then, one by one, they stepped off and swooshed down towards the beach. Even Milton didn't hesitate, though he did keep his eyes shut the whole way.

Or at least he would have if they'd actually made it the whole way.

When they were halfway across, the spaghetti stretched, twisted … and then snapped altogether.

The three children dropped like cannonballs towards the waves below.

But instead of hitting the sea with a splash they landed upright, each standing on something solid.

They looked down to discover they were hitching a lift.

"Sea turtles," laughed Tommy as he struggled to keep his balance.

They skimmed towards the beach like surfers, crouching on the three great green shells as their parrots circled above their heads.

When they reached the shore they hopped off on to the sand.

"We're here!" said Jo as the turtles splashed away further along the beach. "Thanks for the ride!"

"That was a close shave," puffed Milton.

"Now all we need to do is find that

pear tree and the treasure is ours," said Tommy.

Milton pulled the map from his belt and unrolled it.

The hunt was on.

CHAPTER 9

It's not easy to tell different kinds of trees apart in the dark, which is why you never see tree-spotters out at night.

Tommy, Jo, Milton and the parrots were finding that out the hard way.

They came across a lemon tree, a mango tree and a peach tree. But no pear tree.

"Have a look at the map, Milton," said Jo. "What does it say? Are we close?"

"I don't know – it's all dark and stuff," said Milton. "I *think* it might be this one."

Tommy looked up at the tree.

"I can't tell what kind it is. I can't see any pears."

"Throw a stick up and see if you can knock a pear down," suggested Milton.

So Tommy grabbed a piece of driftwood and hurled it into the darkness.

There was a moment of silence, then:

CLONK!

"OUCH!"

"What was that?" said Milton.

"It's definitely not a pear tree," groaned Tommy. "It's a coconut tree.

OOOW."

All seemed lost, when just at that moment the dark clouds parted and a shaft of silvery moonlight shone down on the island.

"I can see the map!" yelped Milton. "The pear tree is next to a huge rock shaped like a skull."

They looked up and down the line of trees. Nothing.

"Where could it be?" said Milton.

Right on cue a breeze rippled across the sea and blew among the palm

leaves and vines. The undergrowth parted and two dark eye sockets peered out at them above a toothy grin.

"There it is!" cried Jo. "The skull of Skull Island!"

They ran over to it as the light from the moon picked out the unmistakable shapes of dozens of shiny green pears hanging from branches.

"This is it!" yelped Jo. "The treasure must be near here."

They looked around. Now where would a pirate bury treasure?

"I'll bet it's under the *skull*!" said Tommy.

They didn't have a spade, so they began digging with their hands. Even the parrots joined in, scooping tiny piles of sand with their beaks.

Down they dug beneath the front of the skull, deeper and deeper, until only their heads could be seen bobbing up and down.

"It isn't here," sighed Jo after a while. "This whole mission has been a big waste of time."

But just as she was about to climb

out of the hole there was a *clunk*.

"Och, my poor wee beak!"

squawked McBeaky.

He had pecked something hard
and wooden.

Everyone scrabbled the sand away a bit more. And there, in the bottom of the hole, was a large wooden chest.

"Treasure!" marvelled Milton.

"Not just any treasure," said Tommy. *"The Lost Treasure of Mandaloo."*

With an almighty heave the three friends wrenched the chest on to the beach.

Tommy looked at Jo and Milton.

"Who's going to open it?" he said.

"We should all do it at the same

time," said Jo.

They huddled round it and put their hands on the lid.

"Everyone ready?" smiled Tommy.

The others nodded, their eyes gleaming with excitement.

"OK. One … two … thr—"

"AAAAAAAARRRRRRRRR,"
said a gravelly voice behind them.

"I'm really, *really* hoping that was McBeaky doing a Captain Firebeard impression," gulped Tommy.

"Wasn't me," croaked McBeaky, who was sitting on his shoulder.

They turned round very slowly. Standing there were all of the teachers

and, in front of them, looking incredibly, **SICKENINGLY** smug were Spiky Spencer, Muttonhead Max and Greta the Grouch.

"We told you they were up to no good, sir," said Spencer. "Look at them, trying to steal the treasure. Little sea slugs."

"We were **NOT** stealing it!" growled Jo. "We just wanted to prove we could find it and have a *real* pirate adventure instead of just learning about it in class!"

Spencer, Muttonhead and Greta the Grouch snorted.

"Well, you'll be walking the plank

now – right out of the school and back home," sneered Spencer.

Captain Firebeard took a step forward, his great beard glowing red in the moonlight.

"I'll be the judge of that," he grizzled. "Looks like you sneaky sea urchins have been very busy while everyone was asleep, eh?"

Tommy, Jo and Milton looked at their feet and mumbled, "Sorry, Captain Firebeard."

"Seems you managed to crack the code, too."

Milton beamed, then remembered he was in trouble and went back to looking queasy.

"Well, I reckons you should open that there chest, now we be here and all."

The three children hesitated, but Sea Dog Steve nodded, so they crouched down and slowly lifted the lid. It opened with a creak.

Inside was the most incredible pile of... "*Paper?*" said Tommy.

"Where's the treasure?" gasped Jo.

"All that scary stuff for nothing," groaned Milton.

Captain Firebeard let out a wheezy chuckle.

"Take a closer look, me hearties," he said.

The three peered at the sheets of elaborately decorated parchment paper.

CERTIFICATE OF
PIRATING PERFECTION Nº1

**This 'ere certificate has been awarded
for sensational swashbuckling skills
and brilliant buccaneering.**

**The pirate pupil what earned this certificate has
shown outstandin' bravery, cleverosity and
treasure sniffin' talent and definitely ain't no
slithery sea slug nor blustering bilge weasel.**
Aaaarrrrrr!

Signed: CAPTAIN M.S. FIREBEARD

"You mean we've really passed our first Pirate test?" said Tommy, grinning as he caught the eyes of his two pals.

"I was hoping someone would have the gumption to search for the treasure when I made up that map," said Captain Firebeard. "And I had an inkling it might be you three."

Spencer and his cronies looked like someone had just poured cold rice pudding down their trousers.

"But, sir!" spluttered Spencer. "I demand that they be punished! This *instant*!"

Captain Firebeard fixed him with a

steely glare. "Another word out of you three piddling pilchards and your next lesson will be *'How To Get Marooned On A Desert Island'.*"

Spencer stopped talking very quickly.

"Now," said the captain. "Everyone back to the *Barnacle* – we've got a proper pirate celebration to prepare for.

"AAARRRRRRRR!"

CHAPTER 10

Tommy checked his chin in the mirror above his locker. Still no beard. He tried a sneaky little squeeze.

"NNNNNGG GGGHHH!"

Nothing.

He sighed. Oh well, he might

not have bushy face-furniture like Captain Firebeard, but after his treasure-hunting adventure he was one boot-step closer to becoming a real pirate.

"How's the beard coming along, Cap'n Baldchin?" said a voice right behind him.

Tommy just about jumped out of his skin.

It was Milton and Jo, laughing their stripy socks off.

"Come on," chuckled Jo. "The ceremony is about to start."

It was the last day of school before the holidays and a grand pirate parade was being held on the deck

of the *Rusty Barnacle*.

The three friends climbed the staircases up through the ship and out into the morning sunshine.

Everyone was already there. The teachers, all of the pupils and, of course, Captain Firebeard himself.

There was even a special area where the parents, who had been invited aboard now the ship was safely tied up back at the harbour, were sitting. Tommy's mum and dad waved when they saw him.

Tommy, Jo and Milton hurried to their places alongside the other pupils, who were all standing proudly in a line under the main mast.

McBeaky, Flash and Wobbles flapped down and landed on their

shoulders as the clock tower in town struck two o'clock.

"Ladeees an' gennelmen," declared Captain Firebeard, striding into the centre of the deck. "Shipmates and pirate pupils, seafarers and landlubbers – welcome to the grand pirate parade."

The parents clapped and the children's chests swelled with pride.

"We've had a whale of a term, with some young pirates coming through who I'd be glad to sing a sea shanty with, not to mention go a-swashbuckling with," continued the captain. "And now it gives me the greatest of pirate pleasures to present the CERTIFICATE OF BUCCANEER BRILLIANCE: LEVEL ONE to all that have passed this first term."

Captain Firebeard went along the line of children and Sea Dog Steve passed him the certificates to hand out, only occasionally getting them skewered on his hook. Maggie Magpie and One-Eyed Norm looked on, smiling proudly. Even Gumms clasped his fish-paste-covered hands together in delight.

Finally, after all the pupils had received their certificates, Captain Firebeard came to Tommy, Jo and Milton. He winked at them and smiled. Or at least they thought he smiled – it was hard to tell under all those red whiskers.

"And last but not least we come to these three starfish," he announced. "They've already had their certificates, by way of a treasure chest, but I have one more thing to award them."

Jo glanced at Tommy, who shrugged. He didn't know what to expect.

Captain Firebeard whistled an old sea shanty tune and his big red parrot, Blaze, swooped down on to his shoulder carrying a leather pouch in his beak.

The Captain opened it and poured three small gold lumps on to his huge palm.

"Every year," he declared, "we present the Pirates' Gold Tooth award to the new pupils what have shown themselves to be destined for great things on the seven seas."

He picked up a tooth and held it up between his big fingers. It glinted in the sunlight.

"You three don't look like you have

any need of a spare tooth just yet, so there's a pin on the back of each one."

He pinned the first tooth to Milton's waistcoat, the next to Jo's and the last one to Tommy's.

"Whizz-kid Milton – Jellylegs don't suit ye now, lad – Jo the Fearless and Hotshot Tom, I be honoured to declare you all this year's Pirate Champions!"

The other pupils whooped and hollered and the parents stood up to applaud the young heroes.

There were only three pirate pupils

who weren't clapping or cheering.

That's because Spiky Spencer, Muttonhead Max and Greta the Grouch were far too busy swabbing

the smelly canteen floor down below. It seemed there was nothing Captain Firebeard liked less than un-piratey sneaky behaviour.

"I'll get those shrimps if it's the last thing I do," sneered Spencer as he heard the noise above.

But Tommy, Jo and Milton were having way too much fun at the pirate parade party to care about what Spiky Spencer thought.

As the sea shanties played and everyone danced and sang on the deck of the *Rusty Barnacle* the three friends huddled together and made a pledge.

"Pirate pals for ever?" said Tommy.

"Pirate pals for ever!"

echoed Jo and Milton.

"Parrot pals for ever!"

squawked their three parrots.

Tommy looked down at the shiny gold tooth pinned to his waistcoat.

"I don't know about you," he said with a smile, "but I'm looking forward to next term already."

THE END

CHAE STRATHIE

Cap'n Chae Strathie regularly sails the Seven Seas in his trusty ship, *The Inky Nib*, shouting "ARRRRRR!" at passing seagulls and writing stories about the pirates he meets on his adventures. He has a black-belt in swashbuckling and timber-shivering and has a parrot called Scribbles. When he is ashore he lives in a village in Fife, Scotland, with a bunch o' landlubbers and some cats. Arrrrrr!

ANNA CHERNYSHOVA

Cap'n Anna Chernyshova is a sea artist through and through. You'll find her in the crow's nest, drawing everything she spies – from slippery sea monsters to blistering barnacles. When she's not adventuring the globe and sketching portraits of famous pirates, she's moored in Cambridge with her family and salty sea dog McStinky.

S+〜🐛**t**   **2**   **tHe**   😠 Grrr **+8**
Sail   to   the   Great

WH+ 👧 ~~g~~ **+** ✋🖌️
Whirlpool

t+ 🐔   **G+** 🖐️~~t~~ ~~e~~
then   go

R+ 🧑~~Kn~~   🐱~~e~~   **THE**   📦~~g~~
right   at   the   old

S+ ✏️~~c~~ **+WR+** 🏆~~n~~   *and*   ⭐~~a~~ **+8**
shipwreck   and   straight

on   **2**   💀   👁️**+L+**✋~~h~~ .
on   to   Skull   Island.

The   🌳~~ee~~ **m +** 📏   **iS**   **h+** 🥛~~L~~ **+d+** 🖊️~~p~~
The   treasure   is   hidden

N+ 👂   *the*   **P+** 🧸~~b~~   **3**~~h~~
near   the   pear   tree